## IMPORTANT TERMS

- **Constitution:** The main set of laws for the United States.

- **Democracy:** A government run by the people, in which individuals can pick their leaders by voting in elections.

- **Discrimination:** The act of treating people unfairly for being part of a certain group.

- **Equality:** The state in which people have the same rights and opportunities no matter who they are, where they come from, or what they believe.

- **Freedom of speech:** A right guaranteed by the Constitution in which people can express their opinions without fear of being punished by the government.

- **Integration:** The practice of bringing together people of diverse backgrounds for equal opportunities.

- **Justice:** Fair treatment. Injustice means unfair treatment.

- **Minister:** A person who performs religious ceremonies.

- **Nonviolence:** The expression of beliefs in a peaceful way.

- **Prejudice:** Hatred of a person or a group for no reason.

- **Protest:** Action taken by a group of people who want to show that they are strongly against something they consider unfair, such as discrimination.

- **Rights:** Freedoms that are guaranteed by the government. Also known as civil rights or equal rights.

- **Segregation:** A kind of discrimination in which one group of people is unfairly kept apart from another.

- **Voting:** The way people in a democracy choose the leaders for their government.

## RESOURCES

- Branch, Taylor. *The King Years: Historic Moments in the Civil Rights Movement.* New York: Simon & Schuster, 2013.

- DuVernay, Ava, dir. *Selma.* Los Angeles: Paramount Pictures, 2014.

- King, Martin Luther, Jr. "I Have a Dream" speech. Animation. Martin Luther King, Jr. Research and Education Institute. Stanford University. https://freedomsring.stanford.edu/?view=Speech.

- King, Martin Luther, Jr. *Stride Toward Freedom: The Montgomery Story.* Boston: Beacon Press, 2010.

- King, Martin Luther, Jr. *Why We Can't Wait.* Boston: Beacon Press, 2011.

- National Geographic Kids. "Hero for All: Martin Luther King, Jr." https://kids.nationalgeographic.com/history/article/martin-luther-king-jr.

- Oates, Stephen B. *Let the Trumpet Sound: A Life of Martin Luther King, Jr.* New York: Harper Perennial, 2013.

# THE INSPIRING LIFE OF MARTIN LUTHER KING, JR.

**January 15, 1929:** Born in Atlanta, Georgia

**1948:** Ordained a Baptist minister, becoming the Reverend Martin Luther King, Jr.

**1953:** Marries fellow activist Coretta Scott

**1955:** Receives a graduate degree in philosophy, becoming the Reverend Doctor Martin Luther King, Jr.; elected leader of the bus boycott in Montgomery, Alabama

**1957:** Forms the Southern Christian Leadership Conference to fight for civil rights

**1963:** Leads a protest against segregation in Birmingham, Alabama; arrested and jailed; writes "Letter from Birmingham Jail"; gives his "I Have a Dream" speech at the March on Washington

**1964:** Becomes the then-youngest person to receive the Nobel Peace Prize

**1965:** Leads a protest in Selma, Alabama, against voting restrictions, ending in a march to Montgomery

**1966:** Fights discrimination in housing, employment, and schools

**1967:** Announces the Poor People's Campaign to help struggling people of all backgrounds

**1968:** Assassinated in Memphis, Tennessee, during a protest for workers' rights

**1983:** National holiday established in his honor

**2011:** Martin Luther King, Jr. Memorial dedicated in Washington, DC

## BE LIKE MARTIN

- Learn everything you can from books.
- Stand up for fairness.
- Help others whenever you can.
- Seek peaceful solutions to problems.
- Treat people with kindness and respect.

## NONVIOLENT CIVIL RIGHTS PROTESTS

- **The March:** Walking from one place to another while singing songs, chanting, and holding signs.
- **The Boycott:** Refusing to buy a product or take part in an activity as a way of ending unfair practices.
- **The Sit-In:** African Americans gathering in a whites-only place to challenge discrimination.
- **The Swim-In:** African Americans swimming in a white-only place to change the rules.

## MARTIN'S WISE WORDS

- "The time is always right to do what is right."
- "Love is the only force capable of transforming an enemy into a friend."
- "Commit yourself to the noble struggle for equal rights. You will make a better person of yourself, a greater nation of your country, and a finer world to live in."

## AUTHOR'S NOTE

In the 1950s and 1960s, **Dr. Martin Luther King, Jr.,** helped lead the civil rights movement to great success. Through his beautiful speeches, brave protests, and powerful books, he challenged the United States' unfair treatment of African Americans.

Martin brought people together in the spirit of friendship. He greeted hatred with love, earning the nickname the Peaceful Warrior.

After the 1965 voting rights march in Selma, Alabama, Martin had even bigger plans for equality and justice—not just for Black people, but for everyone. He hoped to stop war, improve schools, and make sure everyone had good jobs and places to live. As always, he faced threats of violence for his vision of peace. But he did not back down, insisting, "I have a job to do."

On April 4, 1968, a man with a gun ended Martin's life. But no one could stop the movement he helped set in motion. Americans continued to fight for their rights, inspired by his example. In 1983, the United States declared a holiday in his honor every January. And in 2011, the country built a Martin Luther King, Jr. Memorial near the spot where he gave his famous "I Have a Dream" speech at the March on Washington.

To this day, Martin's dream lives on.

## YOU ARE A STAR

Remember how much I admire the Declaration of Independence? At our country's birth in 1776, it proclaimed freedom and equality for everyone. I've worked hard to make the United States live up to this wonderful goal—and I know that you can, too!

We still need to see the good in one another.

We still need to live with each other in peace.

Let us join together and change the world with love.

Let us join together and make my dream come true.

Do YOU have a dream for making the world a better place?

Stand up and speak out. It really works!

## HERE COME THE VOTERS

The Voting Rights Act of 1965 outlawed rules that kept African Americans from voting. It helped thousands of us vote for the first time! Along with the Civil Rights Act of 1964, it aimed to replace segregation with integration: bringing all people together for equal opportunities.

The Selma protest was our movement's greatest victory.

It led to a national voting rights law!

But we still need to do more.

Do you know why?

When African Americans were free to vote, we could choose leaders who shared our values.

In Selma, they quickly voted out that sheriff with his "NEVER" button!

## A CHANGE IS GOING TO COME

In Montgomery, I told the marchers that "the arc of the moral universe is long, but it bends toward justice." Do you know what that means? It was my way of saying that we would win equal rights, even if it took awhile. The harder we worked, the sooner it would happen.

I invited all Americans, from all backgrounds, to join us on the march.

Thousands traveled to Alabama, carrying their own signs and banners.

Maids, students, and movie stars.

Parents pushing baby carriages.

People on canes and crutches.

Coretta and I walked together in front.

Five days later, we reached Montgomery in peace.

"What do we want?" I asked the group.

"FREEDOM!" they shouted.

"When do we want it?" I asked.

"NOW!"

During our march, we sang "We shall overcome . . . some . . . day."

When we made it to Montgomery, we added joyful new words!

## POWER TO THE PEOPLE

The United States is a democracy, which means people pick their own leaders through the act of voting. African Americans wanted to vote like everyone else, but some places used threats and violence to deny us that right.

We gathered in Selma for a march to the state capital in Montgomery.

But Alabama's governor used violence to stop our nonviolent protest.

His troops attacked the marchers on the bridge leading out of town.

That only made us more determined!

A few days later, we set off again on the fifty-mile journey to Montgomery.

Could we make it there safely?

Everyone could see that Selma's sheriff did not want Black people to have equal rights.

During our march, he wore a button that said "NEVER."

## DANCING FOR PEACE

I received a major award called the Nobel Peace Prize for my peaceful fight against prejudice. At the celebration, I took a break from my work to have a little fun. I even got to dance with Coretta!

In 1964, Congress passed the Civil Rights act.

This national law ended segregation in restaurants, swimming pools, and libraries.

Even at drinking fountains!

But I knew we had more work to do.

Many places still had rules to keep Black people from voting.

That's why we called for another nonviolent protest in the Alabama city of Selma.

With all the troubles of the past year, I didn't have many reasons to smile.

That changed on the day the president of the United States signed the Civil Rights Act!

## UNITED WE STAND

The March on Washington brought together people of all races. I was proud to see diverse Americans standing side by side, united in the cause of justice.

In the middle of my speech in Washington, DC, I stopped reading what I had written and spoke from the heart.

*I have a dream that my four little children will one day live in a nation where they will not be judged by the color of their skin but by the content of their character . . .*

*I have a dream that . . . little Black boys and Black girls will be able to join hands with little white boys and white girls as sisters and brothers.*

*I HAVE A DREAM TODAY!*

When I finished, the 250,000 listening made the loudest roar I had ever heard.

My speech seemed to give them hope.

Afterward, more people called for a national law against segregation.

People clapped every time I said, "I HAVE A DREAM."

Men and women in the front row held hands and shouted, "DREAM SOME MORE!"

## THE CHILDREN'S MARCH

Thousands of children came to our march in Birmingham. When the police arrested them, other children came to take their places. The city's leaders could see that African Americans would never give up, so they let all of us out of jail and changed their laws. Another victory for our movement!

Even from jail, I wanted to explain why we would not stop our peaceful protests.

And why it was wrong to arrest us just for speaking out.

So, I wrote the world a letter.

African Americans have waited long enough for equality, I said.

"Oppressed people cannot remain oppressed forever."

Friends snuck my letter out of jail, made copies, and passed it around.

Many people read it and joined our cause.

Even the president of the United States!

But how could I reach all American citizens?

The time had come for my important speech at the March on Washington.

I wrote my letter on the few scraps of paper in my jail cell.

When I ran out of space, I started writing on toilet paper!

## MUSIC TO MARCH BY

At protests, singing lifted our spirits. Our songs spoke of changing the world, like the lovely "We Shall Overcome." "Deep in my heart/I do believe/we shall overcome/some day."

If we could change the laws in Montgomery, maybe we could change them everywhere else.

I was asked to help lead another nonviolent protest in Birmingham, Alabama.

This time, we would demand equal treatment in restaurants and stores.

We would also challenge American leaders to make a national law against segregation.

Hundreds of people came to Birmingham to march, sing, and boycott businesses.

The city ordered us to stop, but we kept speaking out for our rights.

And that's how I ended up in jail.

In troubled times, my wife, Coretta, always stood by me.

And my children always played with me!

## THE POWER OF LOVE

People sent me letters during our fight for equal rights in Montgomery. Some supported our boycott, and some did not. I answered all of them politely, even those who disagreed with me. The best way to work out our differences is with love and respect.

Guess what—we stuck together!

African American men and women in Montgomery kept the boycott going for more than a year.

The whole country learned about it through radio, television, and newspapers.

At last, the city changed its law.

For the first time, Black people could sit anywhere we wanted on Montgomery buses.

The victory gave me an even bolder idea for ending discrimination.

I took a bus to celebrate the end of our boycott.

You can probably figure out where I sat. Right up in front!

## FREEDOM OF SPEECH

Remember how much I admire the US Constitution? It promises rights for all Americans. We have the right to speak out for what we believe in and the right to protest injustice. That made our bus boycott part of a great American tradition called freedom of speech.

African Americans decided to stay off Montgomery's buses until they changed their rules.

This kind of nonviolent protest is called a boycott.

It meant the bus company would lose all the money we usually paid for rides.

Instead, we found other ways to get to work.

We walked, hitchhiked, and carpooled, no matter how much trouble it took.

The city's white leaders expected us to give up our boycott after a week or two.

Would we be tough enough to stick together?

Even senior citizens boycotted, walking for miles instead of taking a bus.

One of them rode to work on a mule!

## A PEACEFUL WAY TO MAKE A POINT

Violence means causing harm, but nonviolence is a way to peacefully challenge discrimination. African Americans could march together, hold up signs, and speak out for equality. If these nonviolent protests made the news, even more people would learn about our cause.

After I finished school, I moved to Montgomery, Alabama, to preach at Dexter Avenue Baptist Church.

The city's laws kept Black people segregated, even on buses.

One day, my friend Rosa Parks grew tired of this treatment.

A white bus driver told her to leave her seat, and she refused.

Then the police came and arrested her.

How could Rosa and I work with others to change this shameful law for Montgomery buses?

With a bold plan.

A nonviolent protest!

Montgomery buses set aside the first few rows for white riders and made African Americans sit in back.

When the back rows filled up, we had to stand in the aisle—even if the front seats were empty!

## FINDING MY VOICE

I liked reading about leaders who inspired people with their ideas. I wanted to do that myself! I worked on learning new words and using them in speeches. I practiced in front of a mirror, wearing my nicest clothes.

I studied to be a minister, like my father.

But I also studied the US Constitution and the Declaration of Independence.

These documents explain what Americans believe in.

Freedom. Equality. Justice for all.

I believed in those things, too.

So, I imagined a bold plan for ending segregation.

It would take a lot of creative thinking—and all the courage I could muster.

In graduate school, I argued with a white classmate who did not believe in equal rights.

I changed his mind, and soon we became friends!

## FROM SLAVERY TO SEGREGATION

Black people were enslaved in America for more than two hundred years, followed by one hundred years of segregation. Segregation meant that white people kept us apart from them in different schools and neighborhoods, all because of our skin color. I dreamed of joining with others to end segregation, including some white people who hated it as much as I did.

I first experienced discrimination as a boy in Atlanta, Georgia.

My father preached at our church, and the African American community respected our family.

But many whites did not respect us—or any other Black people.

They would not let us eat in their restaurants, swim in their pools, or play in their parks.

They would not even let us drink from their water fountains!

Someone had to change these unfair rules.

Why not me?

Even before I started school, I loved books.

They could help me understand injustice—as soon as I learned how to read!

> "I have the pleasure to present to you: DR. MARTIN LUTHER KING, JR."

## MY TIME TO SHINE

On August 28, 1963, the March on Washington demanded equal rights for African Americans. These are also known as civil rights. People from all around the country gathered for a day of music, talks, and prayers. For my turn on stage, I wanted to make a speech that no one would ever forget!

I stood before a huge crowd in Washington, DC.

I started to read my speech but wondered if I had the right words.

What could I say about equality in the United States?

About peace between Black and white people?

About a better future for everyone?

After all my struggles, how could I offer hope?

My parents always told me I could grow up to do something special.

But they never thought I would be THIS famous!

# YOU ARE A STAR, MARTIN LUTHER KING, JR.

WRITTEN BY
DEAN ROBBINS

ILLUSTRATED BY
ANASTASIA MAGLOIRE WILLIAMS

SCHOLASTIC PRESS ★ NEW YORK

For Mary Ann and Andy.

With gratitude to Katie Heit and Marietta Zacker.
—D. Robbins

I dedicate this to the children who dream big and love without fear. Thank you for saving the world with your hope.
—A. M. Williams

Text copyright © 2025 by Dean Robbins

Illustrations copyright © 2025 by Anastasia Magloire Williams

All rights reserved. Published by Scholastic Press, an imprint of Scholastic Inc., *Publishers since 1920*. SCHOLASTIC, SCHOLASTIC PRESS, and associated logos are trademarks and/or registered trademarks of Scholastic Inc.

The publisher does not have any control over and does not assume any responsibility for author or third-party websites or their content.

No part of this publication may be reproduced, stored in a retrieval system, or transmitted in any form or by any means, electronic, mechanical, photocopying, recording, or otherwise, or used to train any artificial intelligence technologies, without written permission of the publisher. For information regarding permission, write to Scholastic Inc., Attention: Permissions Department, 557 Broadway, New York, NY 10012.

Library of Congress Cataloging-in-Publication Data available

ISBN 978-1-338-89510-0 (PB) / 978-1-338-89511-7 (RLB)

10 9 8 7 6 5 4 3 2 1     25 26 27 28 29

Printed in China  38

First edition, January 2025

Book design by Jaime Lucero